THE EVIL SPELL

Emily Arnold McCully

HARPER & ROW, PUBLISHERS

NEW YORK

For Ann and Beany

The Evil Spell
Copyright © 1990 by Emily Arnold McCully

Library of Congress Cataloging-in-Publication Data
McCully, Emily Arnold.
    The evil spell / by Emily Arnold McCully.
        p.   cm.
    Summary: Edwin, an acting bear, gets his first important role in
the family theatre production but is struck with stage fright on
opening night.
    ISBN 0-06-024153-5 : $. — ISBN 0-06-024154-3 (lib. bdg.) :
$
    [1. Stage fright—Fiction.   2. Acting—Fiction.   3. Bears—
Fiction.]   I. Title.
PZ7.M13913Ev 1990   89-24536
[E]—dc20   CIP
                                                          AC

THE
EVIL SPELL

Every year when the Farm Theater opened for a new season,
Edwin would be cast as

the little brother,

 a butler,

one of the soldiers

 or a delivery boy.

His big sister, Zaza, who had already been to Hollywood to try TV, was always the princess, or the doctor's daughter with a mysterious illness. Even his little sister, Sarah, had played an orphan who turned out to be rich.

Edwin knew in his heart that he was ready for an important part too.

Bruno, his father, was preparing to cast the first play of the season, and Sophie, his mother, was designing the sets. Zaza, Sarah and Edwin swept the stage.

"I can't wait to find out who I'm going to be!" said Zaza. "Will I wear a gown? Will I fight a duel?"

"Will I get laughs?" wondered Sarah.

Edwin hardly dared let himself hope. After all, the most important line he had delivered last season was "A handsome stranger asked me to give you this message, Miss."

Finally, Bruno called the family together.

"My new play is called *The Evil Spell*," he said. "It is about a queen, a king and a princess. They are happy until a monster tries to steal all the gold in the palace. The king takes the gold away and hides it.

"To get even, the monster casts an evil spell on the queen and the princess, and they cannot speak or move. The king learns the magic words that break the spell. He saves the queen and the princess, and the monster begs to be forgiven. They forgive her."

"Now," Bruno continued,
"you, Sophie, my dear,
will play the queen."
"Yaaaaay!" shouted the children.

"Sarah will play the princess
and also a knight of the palace."
"Yaaaaay!" cried the children again.

"Zaza will play the monster," said Bruno.
"Oooooooh," said Sarah. Zaza smiled.

Bruno said, "The most important scene in the play is the one where the king says the magic words that break the evil spell."

"And you play the king!" shouted Sarah.

"No. I will play the old wizard who tells the king to hide the gold."

"But who will play the king?" asked Zaza.

Edwin held his breath. He was the only one left. Could it be...?

"And *Edwin* will play the hero-king!" said Bruno. "He is ready for a major role."

Edwin gasped. Zaza said, "Edwin has never played a hero before."

"He can do it," said Sarah.

Edwin was dizzy with joy.

Rehearsals began at once. Edwin threw himself into the role
of the king. When he wasn't in a scene, he liked to stroll out the
stage door and say his big speech—the magic words—to the
birds and butterflies. "O fair queen and precious princess," he
said, "I release you from the evil spell cast by the merciless
monster...."

The sun warmed his fur and he understood just how a hero
feels: bigger than life, brave, generous and strong.

"What a deep voice you have, Edwin," said Sarah one day.

"Edwin, you look about six feet tall," said Zaza. "You are a good king!"

Bruno and Sophie took him aside and said, "Son, you make us proud."

At dress rehearsal, everything went beautifully. The angry monster cast the evil spell, and the queen and the princess were frozen in their tracks. Edwin came on for his big scene. He said his most important speech: "O fair queen and precious princess..." When he had finished, the queen and the princess broke free and embraced him. The monster begged forgiveness. Edwin forgave her.

On opening night, the cast gathered in the dressing room.
Edwin put on his robe and his crown.

"Places!" called Bruno.

While Edwin waited in the wings for his big scene, he practiced his speech one last time. "O fair monster—" he said. *What?* "O fair queen and merciless princess—" *NO!* "O precious monster and fair queen..." *NO!*

Edwin's palms were sweating, his costume was strangling him and his heart was bursting out of his chest! He had never made a mistake before! What was the matter with him?

"Edwin!" Bruno whispered. Onstage, Sophie and Sarah were already frozen in their evil spell. The monster was hissing and growling beside them.

Bruno gave Edwin a little shove. "GO!" he said.

Somehow, Edwin moved his feet. Desperately, he looked back at Bruno, then at Sophie and Sarah. He was supposed to speak, but his mind was completely blank!

The harder Edwin tried to remember his lines, the more frozen he became. Bruno was whispering behind him, but the roaring in Edwin's ears was like waves breaking over a rocky shore. Sophie, Sarah and Zaza looked horrified. Someone in the audience coughed, others began to grumble. Still, Edwin was unable to move or speak.

Bruno shut the curtain. Edwin raced for the stage door.

He ran and ran. Never, ever, could he face anyone again! He had disgraced himself and let his whole family down. "I wanted an important part," he thought, "but I'm not even an actor! I'll have to run away and work at a dump somewhere." He fell under a bush and sobbed.

"Edwin?" It was Sophie. "Oh, Edwin."

"NO!" Edwin cried. Suddenly, he understood what had happened. "Stay away from me! I'm under an evil spell!"

"An evil spell?" asked Sophie.

"Yes! An evil spell made me forget my lines and ruin the whole play!"

Bruno and Sophie smiled. "Oh, darling," said Sophie. "That wasn't an evil spell!"

"No, indeed," said Bruno.

"What was it?" asked Zaza and Sarah.

"That was stage fright!" said Sophie and Bruno.

"Every actor has it sometimes," added Sophie.

"Sophie," said Bruno, "do you remember the time I played Prince Charming? I had such stage fright that I walked off without kissing Sleeping Beauty. She just lay there!"

"*You did that?*" asked Zaza.

"Oh, yes," said Bruno. "It stopped the play."

"Bruno," said Sophie, "do you remember the time I played Madame Zut? I had such stage fright I forgot everyone's fortunes! Finally, they just carried me off!"

"*You too?*" said Sarah.

"Oh, yes," said Sophie.

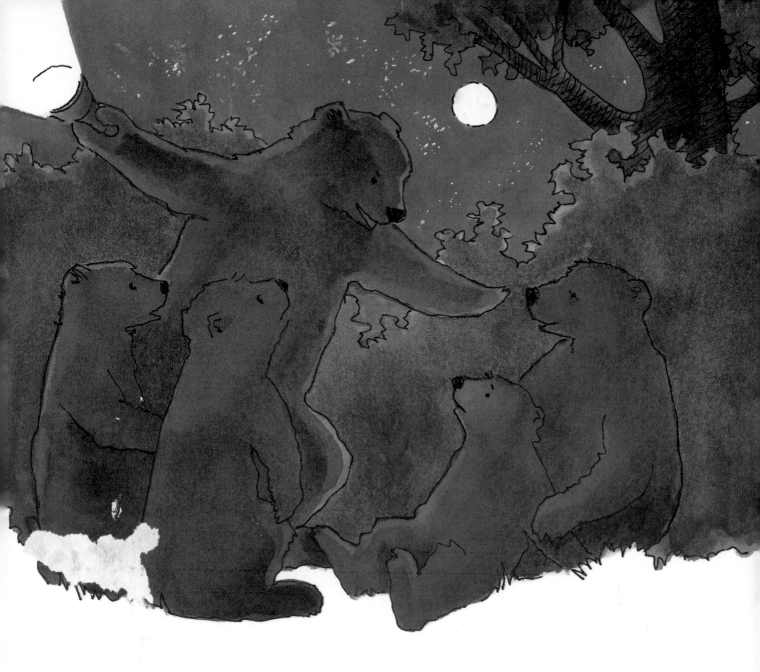

"But it's so awful!" said Edwin. "How do you get rid of stage fright?"

"It's just like any fear," said Bruno. "You mustn't run away. You must try again. We know you're a good actor. You must believe it too. You are the king. The king will do what he is supposed to do."

The next day, to take Edwin's mind off his stage fright, the
family toured Upside Down Falls and had a picnic. Edwin felt
much better until it was time to put on his robe and his crown.
His heart began to pound madly. Was he in the grip of his evil
spell again?

He looked in the dressing-room mirror.

There was the king! Edwin remembered all the times he had rehearsed *The Evil Spell* without a hitch. Then he remembered what Bruno had said: "The king will do what he is supposed to do."

"You are the king," Edwin said to his reflection. "I am an actor who is a king."

He felt bigger than life, brave, generous and strong.

"PLACES!" called Bruno.

Edwin's heart hammered. Was he about to break the evil spell?

The second performance of *The Evil Spell* became famous all over the countryside. "It was magical," said those lucky enough to have seen it. "Young Edwin was a perfect king." All together, there were ten curtain calls.

Edwin had broken the evil spell!